The Tower

W. B. Yeats

CONTENTS

SAILING TO BYZANTIUM

I

That is no country for old men. The young
In one another's arms, birds in the trees,
—Those dying generations—at their song,
The salmon-falls, the mackerel-crowded seas,
Fish flesh or fowl, commend all summer long
Whatever is begotten born and dies.
Caught in that sensual music all neglect
Monuments of unaging intellect.

II

An aged man is but a paltry thing,
A tattered coat upon a stick, unless
Soul clap its hands and sing, and louder sing
For every tatter in its mortal dress,
Nor is there singing school but studying
Monuments of its own magnificence;
And therefore I have sailed the seas and come
To the holy city of Byzantium.

III

O sages standing in God's holy fire
As in the gold mosaic of a wall,
Come from the holy fire, perne in a gyre,
And be the singing masters of my soul.
Consume my heart away; sick with desire

And fastened to a dying animal
It knows not what it is; and gather me
Into the artifice of eternity.

IV

Once out of nature I shall never take
My bodily form from any natural thing,
But such a form as Grecian goldsmiths make
Of hammered gold and gold enamelling
To keep a drowsy emperor awake;
Or set upon a golden bough to sing
To lords and ladies of Byzantium
Of what is past, or passing, or to come.

1927

THE TOWER

I

What shall I do with this absurdity—
O heart, O troubled heart—this caricature,
Decrepit age that has been tied to me
As to a dog's tail? Never had I more
Excited, passionate, fantastical
Imagination, nor an ear and eye
That more expected the impossible—
No, not in boyhood when with rod and fly,
Or the humbler worm, I climbed Ben Bulben's back
And had the livelong summer day to spend.
It seems that I must bid the Muse go pack,
Choose Plato and Plotinus for a friend
Until imagination, ear and eye,
Can be content with argument and deal
In abstract things; or be derided by
A sort of battered kettle at the heel.

II

I pace upon the battlements and stare
On the foundations of a house, or where
Tree, like a sooty finger, starts from the earth;
And send imagination forth
Under the day's declining beam, and call
Images and memories
From ruin or from ancient trees,
For I would ask a question of them all.

Beyond that ridge lived Mrs. French, and once
When every silver candlestick or sconce
Lit up the dark mahogany and the wine,
A serving man that could divine
That most respected lady's every wish,
Ran and with the garden shears
Clipped an insolent farmer's ears
And brought them in a little covered dish.

Some few remembered still when I was young
A peasant girl commended by a song,
Who'd lived somewhere upon that rocky place,
And praised the colour of her face,
And had the greater joy in praising her,
Remembering that, if walked she there,
Farmers jostled at the fair
So great a glory did the song confer.

And certain men, being maddened by those rhymes,
Or else by toasting her a score of times,
Rose from the table and declared it right
To test their fancy by their sight;
But they mistook the brightness of the moon
For the prosaic light of day—
Music had driven their wits astray—
And one was drowned in the great bog of Cloone.

Strange, but the man who made the song was blind,
Yet, now I have considered it, I find
That nothing strange; the tragedy began
With Homer that was a blind man,
And Helen has all living hearts betrayed.
O may the moon and sunlight seem
One inextricable beam,

For if I triumph I must make men mad.
And I myself created Hanrahan
And drove him drunk or sober through the dawn
From somewhere in the neighbouring cottages.
Caught by an old man's juggleries
He stumbled, tumbled, fumbled to and fro
And had but broken knees for hire
And horrible splendour of desire;
I thought it all out twenty years ago:

Good fellows shuffled cards in an old bawn;
And when that ancient ruffian's turn was on
He so bewitched the cards under his thumb
That all, but the one card, became
A pack of hounds and not a pack of cards,
And that he changed into a hare.
Hanrahan rose in frenzy there
And followed up those baying creatures towards—

O towards I have forgotten what—enough!
I must recall a man that neither love
Nor music nor an enemy's clipped ear
Could, he was so harried, cheer;
A figure that has grown so fabulous
There's not a neighbour left to say
When he finished his dog's day:
An ancient bankrupt master of this house.

Before that ruin came, for centuries,
Rough men-at-arms, cross-gartered to the knees
Or shod in iron, climbed the narrow stairs,
And certain men-at-arms there were
Whose images, in the Great Memory stored,
Come with loud cry and panting breast

To break upon a sleeper's rest
While their great wooden dice beat on the board.
As I would question all, come all who can;
Come old, necessitous, half-mounted man;
And bring beauty's blind rambling celebrant;
The red man the juggler sent
Through God-forsaken meadows; Mrs. French,
Gifted with so fine an ear;
The man drowned in a bog's mire,
When mocking muses chose the country wench.

Did all old men and women, rich and poor,
Who trod upon these rocks or passed this door,
Whether in public or in secret rage
As I do now against old age?
But I have found an answer in those eyes
That are impatient to be gone;
Go therefore; but leave Hanrahan
For I need all his mighty memories.

Old lecher with a love on every wind
Bring up out of that deep considering mind
All that you have discovered in the grave,
For it is certain that you have
Reckoned up every unforeknown, unseeing
Plunge, lured by a softening eye,
Or by a touch or a sigh,
Into the labyrinth of another's being;

Does the imagination dwell the most
Upon a woman won or woman lost?
If on the lost, admit you turned aside
From a great labyrinth out of pride,
Cowardice, some silly over-subtle thought
Or anything called conscience once;

And that if memory recur, the sun's
Under eclipse and the day blotted out.

III

It is time that I wrote my will;
I choose upstanding men,
That climb the streams until
The fountain leap, and at dawn
Drop their cast at the side
Of dripping stone; I declare
They shall inherit my pride,
The pride of people that were
Bound neither to Cause nor to State,
Neither to slaves that were spat on,
Nor to the tyrants that spat,
The people of Burke and of Grattan
That gave, though free to refuse—
Pride, like that of the morn,
When the headlong light is loose,
Or that of the fabulous horn,
Or that of the sudden shower
When all streams are dry,
Or that of the hour
When the swan must fix his eye
Upon a fading gleam,
Float out upon a long
Last reach of glittering stream
And there sing his last song.
And I declare my faith;
I mock Plotinus' thought
And cry in Plato's teeth,
Death and life were not
Till man made up the whole,

Made lock, stock and barrel
Out of his bitter soul,
Aye, sun and moon and star, all,
And further add to that
That, being dead, we rise,
Dream and so create
Translunar Paradise.
I have prepared my peace
With learned Italian things
And the proud stones of Greece,
Poet's imaginings
And memories of love,
Memories of the words of women,
All those things whereof
Man makes a superhuman,
Mirror-resembling dream.

As at the loophole there,
The daws chatter and scream,
And drop twigs layer upon layer.
When they have mounted up,
The mother bird will rest
On their hollow top,
And so warm her wild nest.

I leave both faith and pride
To young upstanding men
Climbing the mountain side,
That under bursting dawn
They may drop a fly;
Being of that metal made
Till it was broken by
This sedentary trade.

Now shall I make my soul
Compelling it to study

In a learned school
Till the wreck of body
Slow decay of blood,
Testy delirium
Or dull decrepitude,
Or what worse evil come—
The death of friends, or death
Of every brilliant eye
That made a catch in the breath—
Seem but the clouds of the sky
When the horizon fades;
Or a bird's sleepy cry
Among the deepening shades.

1926

MEDITATIONS IN TIME
OF CIVIL WAR

I

ANCESTRAL HOUSES

Surely among a rich man's flowering lawns,
Amid the rustle of his planted hills,
Life overflows without ambitious pains;
And rains down life until the basin spills,
And mounts more dizzy high the more it rains
As though to choose whatever shape it wills
And never stoop to a mechanical,
Or servile shape, at others' beck and call.

Mere dreams, mere dreams! Yet Homer had not sung
Had he not found it certain beyond dreams
That out of life's own self-delight had sprung
The abounding glittering jet; though now it seems
As if some marvellous empty sea-shell flung
Out of the obscure dark of the rich streams,
And not a fountain, were the symbol which
Shadows the inherited glory of the rich.

Some violent bitter man, some powerful man
Called architect and artist in, that they,
Bitter and violent men, might rear in stone
The sweetness that all longed for night and day,
The gentleness none there had ever known;

But when the master's buried mice can play,
And maybe the great-grandson of that house,
For all its bronze and marble,'s but a mouse.

Oh, what if gardens where the peacock strays
With delicate feet upon old terraces,
Or else all Juno from an urn displays
Before the indifferent garden deities;
Oh, what if levelled lawns and gravelled ways
Where slippered Contemplation finds his ease
And Childhood a delight for every sense,
But take our greatness with our violence!

What if the glory of escutcheoned doors,
And buildings that a haughtier age designed,
The pacing to and fro on polished floors
Amid great chambers and long galleries, lined
With famous portraits of our ancestors;
What if those things the greatest of mankind,
Consider most to magnify, or to bless,
But take our greatness with our bitterness!

II

MY HOUSE

An ancient bridge, and a more ancient tower,
A farmhouse that is sheltered by its wall,
An acre of stony ground,
Where the symbolic rose can break in flower,
Old ragged elms, old thorns innumerable,
The sound of the rain or sound
Of every wind that blows;
The stilted water-hen
Crossing stream again
Scared by the splashing of a dozen cows;

A winding stair, a chamber arched with stone,
A grey stone fireplace with an open hearth,
A candle and written page.
Il Penseroso's Platonist toiled on
In some like chamber, shadowing forth
How the daemonic rage
Imagined everything.
Benighted travellers
From markets and from fairs
Have seen his midnight candle glimmering.

Two men have founded here. A man-at-arms
Gathered a score of horse and spent his days
In this tumultuous spot,
Where through long wars and sudden night alarms
His dwindling score and he seemed cast-a-ways
Forgetting and forgot;
And I, that after me
My bodily heirs may find,

To exalt a lonely mind,
Befitting emblems of adversity.

III

MY TABLE

Two heavy tressels, and a board
Where Sato's gift, a changeless sword,
By pen and paper lies,
That it may moralise
My days out of their aimlessness.
A bit of an embroidered dress
Covers its wooden sheath.
Chaucer had not drawn breath
When it was forged. In Sato's house,
Curved like new moon, moon luminous
It lay five hundred years.
Yet if no change appears
No moon; only an aching heart
Conceives a changeless work of art.
Our learned men have urged
That when and where 'twas forged
A marvellous accomplishment,
In painting or in pottery, went
From father unto son
And through the centuries ran
And seemed unchanging like the sword.
Soul's beauty being most adored,
Men and their business took

The soul's unchanging look;
For the most rich inheritor,
Knowing that none could pass heaven's door
That loved inferior art,
Had such an aching heart
That he, although a country's talk
For silken clothes and stately walk,
Had waking wits; it seemed
Juno's peacock screamed.

IV

MY DESCENDANTS

Having inherited a vigorous mind
From my old fathers I must nourish dreams
And leave a woman and a man behind
As vigorous of mind, and yet it seems
Life scarce can cast a fragrance on the wind,
Scarce spread a glory to the morning beams,
But the torn petals strew the garden plot;
And there's but common greenness after that.

And what if my descendants lose the flower
Through natural declension of the soul,
Through too much business with the passing hour,
Through too much play, or marriage with a fool?
May this laborious stair and this stark tower
Become a roofless ruin that the owl

May build in the cracked masonry and cry
Her desolation to the desolate sky.

The Primum Mobile that fashioned us
Has made the very owls in circles move;
And I, that count myself most prosperous,
Seeing that love and friendship are enough,
For an old neighbour's friendship chose the house
And decked and altered it for a girl's love,
And know whatever flourish and decline
These stones remain their monument and mine.

V

THE ROAD AT MY DOOR

An affable Irregular,
A heavily built Falstaffian man,
Comes cracking jokes of civil war
As though to die by gunshot were
The finest play under the sun.

A brown Lieutenant and his men,
Half dressed in national uniform,
Stand at my door, and I complain
Of the foul weather, hail and rain,
A pear tree broken by the storm.

I count those feathered balls of soot
The moor-hen guides upon the stream,

To silence the envy in my thought;
And turn towards my chamber, caught
In the cold snows of a dream.

VI

THE STARE'S NEST BY MY WINDOW

The bees build in the crevices
Of loosening masonry, and there
The mother birds bring grubs and flies.
My wall is loosening; honey-bees
Come build in the empty house of the stare.

We are closed in, and the key is turned
On our uncertainty; somewhere
A man is killed, or a house burned,
Yet no clear fact to be discerned:
Come build in the empty house of the stare.

A barricade of stone or of wood;
Some fourteen days of civil war;
Last night they trundled down the road
That dead young soldier in his blood:
Come build in the empty house of the stare.

We had fed the heart on fantasies,
The heart's grown brutal from the fare,
More substance in our enmities
Than in our love; oh, honey-bees
Come build in the empty house of the stare.

VII

I SEE PHANTOMS OF HATRED AND OF THE HEART'S FULLNESS AND OF THE COMING EMPTINESS

I climb to the tower top and lean upon broken stone,
A mist that is like blown snow is sweeping over all,
Valley, river, and elms, under the light of a moon
That seems unlike itself, that seems unchangeable,
A glittering sword out of the east. A puff of wind
And those white glimmering fragments of the mist
sweep by.
Frenzies bewilder, reveries perturb the mind;
Monstrous familiar images swim to the mind's eye.

'Vengeance upon the murderers,' the cry goes up,
'Vengeance for Jacques Molay.' In cloud-pale rags,
or in lace,
The rage driven, rage tormented, and rage hungry troop,
Trooper belabouring trooper, biting at arm or at face,
Plunges towards nothing, arms and fingers spreading wide
For the embrace of nothing; and I, my wits astray
Because of all that senseless tumult, all but cried
For vengeance on the murderers of Jacques Molay.

Their legs long delicate and slender, aquamarine their eyes,
Magical unicorns bear ladies on their backs,
The ladies close their musing eyes. No prophecies,
Remembered out of Babylonian almanacs,
Have closed the ladies' eyes, their minds are but a pool
Where even longing drowns under its own excess;
Nothing but stillness can remain when hearts are full
Of their own sweetness, bodies of their loveliness.

The cloud-pale unicorns, the eyes of aquamarine,
The quivering half-closed eyelids, the rags of cloud
or of lace,
Or eyes that rage has brightened, arms it has made lean,
Give place to an indifferent multitude, give place
To brazen hawks. Nor self-delighting reverie,
Nor hate of what's to come, nor pity for what's gone,
Nothing but grip of claw, and the eye's complacency,
The innumerable clanging wings that have put out
the moon.

I turn away and shut the door, and on the stair
Wonder how many times I could have proved my worth
In something that all others understand or share;
But oh, ambitious heart had such a proof drawn forth
A company of friends, a conscience set at ease,
It had but made us pine the more. The abstract joy,
The half read wisdom of daemonic images,
Suffice the ageing man as once the growing boy.

1923

NINETEEN HUNDRED
AND NINETEEN

I

Many ingenious lovely things are gone
That seemed sheer miracle to the multitude,
Protected from the circle of the moon
That pitches common things about. There stood
Amid the ornamental bronze and stone
An ancient image made of olive wood—
And gone are Phidias' famous ivories
And all the golden grasshoppers and bees.

We too had many pretty toys when young;
A law indifferent to blame or praise,
To bribe or threat; habits that made old wrong
Melt down, as it were wax in the sun's rays;
Public opinion ripening for so long
We thought it would outlive all future days.
O what fine thought we had because we thought
That the worst rogues and rascals had died out.

All teeth were drawn, all ancient tricks unlearned,
And a great army but a showy thing;
What matter that no cannon had been turned
Into a ploughshare; parliament and king
Thought that unless a little powder burned
The trumpeters might burst with trumpeting
And yet it lack all glory; and perchance
The guardsmen's drowsy chargers would not prance.

Now days are dragon-ridden, the nightmare
Rides upon sleep: a drunken soldiery
Can leave the mother, murdered at her door,
To crawl in her own blood, and go scot-free;
The night can sweat with terror as before
We pieced our thoughts into philosophy,
And planned to bring the world under a rule,
Who are but weasels fighting in a hole.

He who can read the signs nor sink unmanned
Into the half-deceit of some intoxicant
From shallow wits; who knows no work can stand,
Whether health, wealth or peace of mind were spent
On master work of intellect or hand,
No honour leave its mighty monument,
Has but one comfort left: all triumph would
But break upon his ghostly solitude.

But is there any comfort to be found?
Man is in love and loves what vanishes,
What more is there to say? That country round
None dared admit, if such a thought were his,
Incendiary or bigot could be found
To burn that stump on the Acropolis,
Or break in bits the famous ivories
Or traffic in the grasshoppers or bees?

II

When Loie Fuller's Chinese dancers enwound
A shining web, a floating ribbon of cloth,
It seemed that a dragon of air
Had fallen among dancers, had whirled them round

Or hurried them off on its own furious path;
So the platonic year
Whirls out new right and wrong,
Whirls in the old instead;
All men are dancers and their tread
Goes to the barbarous clangour of gong.

III

Some moralist or mythological poet
Compares the solitary soul to a swan;
I am satisfied with that,
Satisfied if a troubled mirror show it
Before that brief gleam of its life be gone,
An image of its state;
The wings half spread for flight,
The breast thrust out in pride
Whether to play, or to ride
Those winds that clamour of approaching night.

A man in his own secret meditation
Is lost amid the labyrinth that he has made
In art or politics;
Some platonist affirms that in the station
Where we should cast off body and trade
The ancient habit sticks,
And that if our works could
But vanish with our breath
That were a lucky death,
For triumph can but mar our solitude.

The swan has leaped into the desolate heaven:
That image can bring wildness, bring a rage

To end all things, to end
What my laborious life imagined, even
The half imagined, the half written page;
O but we dreamed to mend
Whatever mischief seemed
To afflict mankind, but now
That winds of winter blow
Learn that we were crack-pated when we dreamed.

IV

We, who seven years ago
Talked of honour and of truth,
Shriek with pleasure if we show
The weasel's twist, the weasel's tooth.

V

Come let us mock at the great
That had such burdens on the mind
And toiled so hard and late
To leave some monument behind,
Nor thought of the levelling wind.

Come let us mock at the wise;
With all those calendars whereon
They fixed old aching eyes,
They never saw how seasons run,
And now but gape at the sun.

Come let us mock at the good
That fancied goodness might be gay,
And sick of solitude
Might proclaim a holiday:
Wind shrieked—and where are they?

Mock mockers after that
That would not lift a hand maybe
To help good, wise or great
To bar that foul storm out, for we
Traffic in mockery.

VI

Violence upon the roads: violence of horses;
Some few have handsome riders, are garlanded
On delicate sensitive ear or tossing mane,
But wearied running round and round in their courses
All break and vanish, and evil gathers head:
Herodias' daughters have returned again
A sudden blast of dusty wind and after
Thunder of feet, tumult of images,
Their purpose in the labyrinth of the wind;
And should some crazy hand dare touch a daughter
All turn with amorous cries, or angry cries,
According to the wind, for all are blind.
But now wind drops, dust settles; thereupon
There lurches past, his great eyes without thought
Under the shadow of stupid straw-pale locks,
That insolent fiend Robert Artisson
To whom the love-lorn Lady Kyteler brought
Bronzed peacock feathers, red combs of her cocks.

1919

THE WHEEL

Through winter-time we call on spring,
And through the spring on summer call,
And when abounding hedges ring
Declare that winter's best of all;
And after that there s nothing good
Because the spring-time has not come —
Nor know that what disturbs our blood
Is but its longing for the tomb.

YOUTH AND AGE

Much did I rage when young,
Being by the world oppressed,
But now with flattering tongue
It speeds the parting guest.

1924

THE NEW FACES

If you, that have grown old, were the first dead,
Neither catalpa tree nor scented lime
Should hear my living feet, nor would I tread
Where we wrought that shall break the teeth of time.
Let the new faces play what tricks they will
In the old rooms; night can outbalance day,
Our shadows rove the garden gravel still,
The living seem more shadowy than they.

A PRAYER FOR MY SON

Bid a strong ghost stand at the head
That my Michael may sleep sound,
Nor cry, nor turn in the bed
Till his morning meal come round;
And may departing twilight keep
All dread afar till morning's back,
That his mother may not lack
Her fill of sleep.

Bid the ghost have sword in fist:
Some there are, for I avow
Such devilish things exist,
Who have planned his murder for they know
Of some most haughty deed or thought
That waits upon his future days,
And would through hatred of the bays
Bring that to nought.

Though You can fashion everything
From nothing every day, and teach
The morning stars to sing,
You have lacked articulate speech
To tell Your simplest want, and known,
Wailing upon a woman's knee,
All of that worst ignominy
Of flesh and bone;

And when through all the town there ran
The servants of Your enemy,
A woman and a man,
Unless the Holy Writings lie,
Hurried through the smooth and rough

And through the fertile and waste,
Protecting, till the danger past,
With human love.

TWO SONGS FROM A PLAY

I

I saw a staring virgin stand
Where holy Dionysus died,
And tear the heart out of his side,
And lay the heart upon her hand
And bear that beating heart away;
And then did all the Muses sing
Of Magnus Annus at the spring,
As though God's death were but a play.

Another Troy must rise and set,
Another lineage feed the crow,
Another Argo's painted prow
Drive to a flashier bauble yet.
The Roman Empire stood appalled:
It dropped the reins of peace and war
When that fierce virgin and her Star
Out of the fabulous darkness called.

II

In pity for man's darkening thought
He walked that room and issued thence
In Galilean turbulence;
The Babylonian Starlight brought
A fabulous, formless darkness in;
Odour of blood when Christ was slain
Made Plato's tolerance in vain
And vain the Doric discipline.

WISDOM

The true faith discovered was
When painted panel, statuary,
Glass-mosaic, window-glass,
Straightened all that went awry
When some peasant gospeller
Imagined Him upon the floor
Of a working-carpenter.
Miracle had its playtime where
In damask clothed and on a seat,
Chryselephantine, cedar boarded,
His majestic Mother sat
Stitching at a purple hoarded,
That He might be nobly breeched,
In starry towers of Babylon
Noah's freshet never reached.
King Abundance got Him on
Innocence; and Wisdom He.
That cognomen sounded best
Considering what wild infancy
Drove horror from His Mother's breast.

LEDA AND THE SWAN

A sudden blow: the great wings beating still
Above the staggering girl, her thighs caressed
By the dark webs, her nape caught in his bill,
He holds her helpless breast upon his breast.

How can those terrified vague fingers push
The feathered glory from her loosening thighs?
And how can body, laid in that white rush
But feel the strange heart beating where it lies?

A shudder in the loins engenders there
The broken wall, the burning roof and tower
And Agamemnon dead.
Being so caught up,
So mastered by the brute blood of the air,
Did she put on his knowledge with his power
Before the indifferent beak could let her drop?

1928

ON A PICTURE OF A BLACK CENTAUR

BY EDMOND DULAC

Your hooves have stamped at the black margin of the wood,
Even where horrible green parrots call and swing.
My works are all stamped down into the sultry mud.
I knew that horse play, knew it for a murderous thing.
What wholesome sun has ripened is wholesome food to eat
And that alone; yet I, being driven half insane
Because of some green wing, gathered old mummy wheat
In the mad abstract dark and ground it grain by grain
And after baked it slowly in an oven; but now
I bring full flavoured wine out of a barrel found
Where seven Ephesian topers slept and never knew
When Alexander's empire past, they slept so sound.
Stretch out your limbs and sleep a long Saturnian sleep;
I have loved you better than my soul for all my words,
And there is none so fit to keep a watch and keep
Unwearied eyes upon those horrible green birds.

AMONG SCHOOL CHILDREN

I

I walk through the long schoolroom questioning,
A kind old nun in a white hood replies;
The children learn to cipher and to sing,
To study reading-books and history,
To cut and sew, be neat in everything
In the best modern way—the children's eyes
In momentary wonder stare upon
A sixty year old smiling public man.

II

I dream of a Ledæan body, bent
Above a sinking fire, a tale that she
Told of a harsh reproof, or trivial event
That changed some childish day to tragedy—
Told, and it seemed that our two natures blent
Into a sphere from youthful sympathy,
Or else, to alter Plato's parable,
Into the yolk and white of the one shell.

III

And thinking of that fit of grief or rage
I look upon one child or t'other there
And wonder if she stood so at that age—

For even daughters of the swan can share
Something of every paddler's heritage—
And had that colour upon cheek or hair
And thereupon my heart is driven wild:
She stands before me as a living child.

IV

Her present image floats in to the mind—
Did quattrocento finger fashion it
Hollow of cheek as though it drank the wind
And took a mass of shadows for its meat?
And I though never of Ledæan kind
Had pretty plumage once—enough of that,
Better to smile on all that smile, and show
There is a comfortable kind of old scarecrow.

V

What youthful mother, a shape upon her lap
Honey of generation had betrayed,
And that must sleep, shriek, struggle to escape
As recollection or the drug decide,
Would think her son, did she but see that shape
With sixty or more winters on its head,
A compensation for the pang of his birth,
Or the uncertainty of his setting forth?

VI

Plato thought nature but a spume that plays
Upon a ghostly paradigm of things;
Solider Aristotle played the taws
Upon the bottom of a king of kings;
World-famous golden-thighed Pythagoras
Fingered upon a fiddle stick or strings
What a star sang and careless Muses heard:
Old clothes upon old sticks to scare a bird.

VII

Both nuns and mothers worship images,
But those the candles light are not as those
That animate a mother's reveries,
But keep a marble or a bronze repose.
And yet they too break hearts—O Presences
That passion, piety or affection knows,
And that all heavenly glory symbolise—
O self-born mockers of man's enterprise;

VIII

Labour is blossoming or dancing where
The body is not bruised to pleasure soul,
Nor beauty born out of its own despair,
Nor blear-eyed wisdom out of midnight oil.
O chestnut tree, great rooted blossomer,
Are you the leaf, the blossom or the bole?
O body swayed to music, O brightening glance,
How can we know the dancer from the dance?

COLONUS' PRAISE

(From 'Oedipus at Colonus')

CHORUS

Come praise Colonus' horses and come praise
The wine dark of the wood's intricacies,
The nightingale that deafens daylight there,
If daylight ever visit where,
Unvisited by tempest or by sun,
Immortal ladies tread the ground
Dizzy with harmonious sound,
Semele's lad a gay companion.

And yonder in the gymnasts' garden thrives
The self-sown, self-begotten shape that gives
Athenian intellect its mastery,
Even the grey-leaved olive tree
Miracle-bred out of the living stone;
Nor accident of peace nor war
Shall wither that old marvel, for
The great grey-eyed Athene stares thereon.

Who comes into this country, and has come
Where golden crocus and narcissus bloom,
Where the Great Mother, mourning for her daughter
And beauty-drunken by the water
Glittering among grey-leaved olive trees,
Has plucked a flower and sung her loss;
Who finds abounding Cephisus
Has found the loveliest spectacle there is.

Because this country has a pious mind
And so remembers that when all mankind
But trod the road, or paddled by the shore,
Poseidon gave it bit and oar,
Every Colonus lad or lass discourses
Of that oar and of that bit;
Summer and winter, day and night,
Of horses and horses of the sea, white horses.

THE HERO, THE GIRL,
AND THE FOOL

The Girl

I rage at my own image in the glass,
That's so unlike myself that when you praise it
It is as though you praised another, or even
Mocked me with praise of my mere opposite;
And when I wake towards morn I dread myself
For the heart cries that what deception wins
Cruelty must keep; therefore be warned and go
If you have seen that image and not the woman.

The Hero

I have raged at my own strength because you have loved it.

The Girl

If you are no more strength than I am beauty
I had better find a convent and turn nun;
A nun at least has all men's reverence
And needs no cruelty.

The Hero

I have heard one say
That men have reverence for their holiness
And not themselves.

The Girl

Say on and say
That only God has loved us for ourselves,
But what care I that long for a man's love?

The Fool by the Roadside

When my days that have
From cradle run to grave
From grave to cradle run instead;
When thoughts that a fool
Has wound upon a spool
Are but loose thread, are but loose thread.

When cradle and spool are past
And I mere shade at last
Coagulate of stuff
Transparent like the wind,
I think that I may find
A faithful love, a faithful love.

OWEN AHERN

AND

HIS DANCERS

I

A strange thing surely that my heart when love had
come unsought
Upon the Norman upland or in that poplar shade,
Should find no burden but itself and yet should be
worn out.
It could not bear that burden and therefore it went mad.

The south wind brought it longing, and the east
wind despair,
The west wind made it pitiful, and the north wind afraid.
It feared to give its love a hurt with all the tempest there;
It feared the hurt that she could give and therefore it
went mad.

I can exchange opinion with any neighbouring mind,
I have as healthy flesh and blood as any rhymer's had,
But oh my Heart could bear no more when the upland
caught the wind;
I ran, I ran, from my love's side because my Heart
went mad.

II

The Heart behind its rib laughed out, 'You have called me
mad,' it said.

'Because I made you turn away and run from that
young child;
How could she mate with fifty years that was so
wildly bred?
Let the cage bird and the cage bird mate and the wild bird
mate in the wild.'

'You but imagine lies all day, O murderer,' I replied.
'And all those lies have but one end poor wretches to betray;
I did not find in any cage the woman at my side.
O but her heart would break to learn my thoughts are
far away.'

'Speak all your mind,' my Heart sang out, 'speak all your
mind; who cares,
Now that your tongue cannot persuade the child till
she mistake
Her childish gratitude for love and match your fifty years.
O let her choose a young man now and all for his wild sake.'

A MAN YOUNG AND OLD

FIRST LOVE

Though nurtured like the sailing moon
In beauty's murderous brood,
She walked awhile and blushed awhile
And on my pathway stood
Until I thought her body bore
A heart of flesh and blood.

But since I laid a hand thereon
And found a heart of stone
I have attempted many things
And not a thing is done,
For every hand is lunatic
That travels on the moon.

She smiled and that transfigured me
And left me but a lout,
Maundering here, and maundering there,
Emptier of thought
Than heavenly circuit of its stars
When the moon sails out.

HUMAN DIGNITY

Like the moon her kindness is,
If kindness I may call
What has no comprehension in't,
But is the same for all
As though my sorrow were a scene
Upon a painted wall.

So like a bit of stone I lie
Under a broken tree.
I could recover if I shrieked
My heart's agony
To passing bird, but I am dumb
From human dignity.

THE MERMAID

A mermaid found a swimming lad,
Picked him for her own,
Pressed her body to his body,
Laughed; and plunging down
Forgot in cruel happiness
That even lovers drown.

THE DEATH OF THE HARE

I have pointed out the yelling pack,
The hare leap to the wood,
And when I pass a compliment
Rejoice as lover should
At the drooping of an eye
At the mantling of the blood.

Then suddenly my heart is wrung
By her distracted air
And I remember wildness lost
And after, swept from there,
Am set down standing in the wood
At the death of the hare.

THE EMPTY CUP

A crazy man that found a cup,
When all but dead of thirst,
Hardly dared to wet his mouth
Imagining, moon accursed,
That another mouthful
And his beating heart would burst.
October last I found it too
But found it dry as bone,
And for that reason am I crazed
And my sleep is gone.

HIS MEMORIES

We should be hidden from their eyes,
Being but holy shows
And bodies broken like a thorn
Whereon the bleak north blows,
To think of buried Hector
And that none living knows.

The women take so little stock
In what I do or say
They'd sooner leave their cosseting
To hear a jackass bray;
My arms are like the twisted thorn
And yet there beauty lay;

The first of all the tribe lay there
And did such pleasure take—
She who had brought great Hector down
And put all Troy to wreck—
That she cried into this ear
Strike me if I shriek.

THE FRIENDS OF HIS YOUTH

Laughter not time destroyed my voice
And put that crack in it,
And when the moon's pot-bellied
I get a laughing fit,
For that old Madge comes down the lane
A stone upon her breast,
And a cloak wrapped about the stone,
And she can get no rest
With singing hush and hush-a-bye;
She that has been wild
And barren as a breaking wave
Thinks that the stone's a child.
And Peter that had great affairs
And was a pushing man
Shrieks, 'I am King of the Peacocks,'
And perches on a stone;
And then I laugh till tears run down
And the heart thumps at my side,
Remembering that her shriek was love
And that he shrieks from pride.

SUMMER AND SPRING

We sat under an old thorn-tree
And talked away the night,
Told all that had been said or done
Since first we saw the light,
And when we talked of growing up
Knew that we'd halved a soul
And fell the one in t'other's arms
That we might make it whole;
Then Peter had a murdering look
For it seemed that he and she
Had spoken of their childish days
Under that very tree.
O what a bursting out there was,
And what a blossoming,
When we had all the summer time
And she had all the spring.

THE SECRETS OF THE OLD

I have old women's secrets now
That had those of the young;
Madge tells me what I dared not think
When my blood was strong,
And what had drowned a lover once
Sounds like an old song.

Though Margery is stricken dumb
If thrown in Madge's way,
We three make up a solitude;
For none alive to-day
Can know the stories that we know
Or say the things we say:
How such a man pleased women most
Of all that are gone,

How such a pair loved many years
And such a pair but one,
Stories of the bed of straw
Or the bed of down.

HIS WILDNESS

O bid me mount and sail up there
Amid the cloudy wrack,
For Peg and Meg and Paris' love
That had so straight a back,
Are gone away, and some that stay,
Have changed their silk for sack.

Were I but there and none to hear
I'd have a peacock cry
For that is natural to a man
That lives in memory,
Being all alone I'd nurse a stone
And sing it lullaby.

THE THREE MONUMENTS

They hold their public meetings where
Our most renowned patriots stand,
One among the birds of the air,
A stumpier on either hand;
And all the popular statesmen say
That purity built up the state
And after kept it from decay;
Admonish us to cling to that
And let all base ambition be,
For intellect would make us proud
And pride bring in impurity:
The three old rascals laugh aloud.

FROM 'OEDIPUS AT COLONUS'

I

Endure what life God gives and ask no longer span;
Cease to remember the delights of youth, travel-wearied
aged man; Cease to remember the delights of youth, travel-
wearied aged man;
Delight becomes death-longing if all longing else be vain.

II

Even from that delight memory treasures so,
Death, despair, division of families, all entanglements of
mankind grow,
As that old wandering beggar and these God-hated
children know.

III

In the long echoing street the laughing dancers throng,
The bride is carried to the bridegroom's chamber through
torchlight and tumultuous song;
I celebrate the silent kiss that ends short life or long.

IV

Never to have lived is best, ancient writers say;
Never to have drawn the breath of life, never to have looked
into the eye of day;
The second best's a gay goodnight and quickly turn away.

THE GIFT OF HARUN AL-RASHID

Kusta ben Luka is my name, I write
To Abd Al-Rabban; fellow roysterer once,
Now the good Caliph's learned Treasurer,
And for no ear but his. Carry this letter
Through the great gallery of the Treasure House
Where banners of the Caliphs hang, night-coloured
But brilliant as the night's embroidery,
And wait war's music; pass the little gallery;
Pass books of learning from Byzantium
Written in gold upon a purple stain,
And pause at last, I was about to say,
At the great book of Sappho's song; but no,
For should you leave my letter there, a boy's
Love-lorn, indifferent hands might come upon it
And let it fall unnoticed to the floor.
Pause at the Treatise of Parmenides
And hide it there, for Caliphs to world's end
Must keep that perfect, as they keep her song
So great its fame. When fitting time has passed
The parchment will disclose to some learned man
A mystery that else had found no chronicler
But the wild Bedouin. Though I approve
Those wanderers that welcomed in their tents
What great Harun Al-Rashid, occupied
With Persian embassy or Grecian war,
Must needs neglect; I cannot hide the truth
That wandering in a desert, featureless
As air under a wing, can give birds' wit.
In after time they will speak much of me
And speak but phantasy. Recall the year
When our beloved Caliph put to death
His Vizir Jaffer for an unknown reason;

'If but the shirt upon my body knew it
I'd tear it off and throw it in the fire.'
That speech was all that the town knew, but he
Seemed for a while to have grown young again;
Seemed so on purpose, muttered Jaffer's friends,
That none might know that he was conscience struck—
But that's a traitor's thought. Enough for me
That in the early summer of the year
The mightiest of the princes of the world
Came to the least considered of his courtiers;
Sat down upon the fountain's marble edge
One hand amid the goldfish in the pool;
And thereupon a colloquy took place
That I commend to all the chroniclers
To show how violent great hearts can lose
Their bitterness and find the honey-comb.
'I have brought a slender bride into the house;
You know the saying "Change the bride with Spring",
And she and I, being sunk in happiness,
Cannot endure to think you tread these paths,
When evening stirs the jasmine, and yet
Are brideless.' 'I am falling into years.'

'But such as you and I do not seem old
Like men who live by habit. Every day
I ride with falcon to the river's edge
Or carry the ringed mail upon my back,
Or court a woman; neither enemy,
Game-bird, nor woman does the same thing twice;
And so a hunter carries in the eye
A mimicry of youth. Can poet's thought
That springs from body and in body falls
Like this pure jet, now lost amid blue sky
Now bathing lily leaf and fishes' scale,
Be mimicry?'

'What matter if our souls
Are nearer to the surface of the body
Than souls that start no game and turn no rhyme!
The soul's own youth and not the body's youth
Shows through our lineaments. My candle's bright,
My lantern is too loyal not to show
That it was made in your great father's reign.'

'And yet the jasmine season warms our blood.'

'Great prince, forgive the freedom of my speech;
You think that love has seasons, and you think
That if the spring bear off what the spring gave
The heart need suffer no defeat; but I
Who have accepted the Byzantine faith,
That seems unnatural to Arabian minds,
Think when I choose a bride I choose for ever;
And if her eye should not grow bright for mine
Or brighten only for some younger eye,
My heart could never turn from daily ruin,
Nor find a remedy.' 'But what if I
Have lit upon a woman, who so shares
Your thirst for those old crabbed mysteries,
So strains to look beyond our life, an eye
That never knew that strain would scarce seem bright,
And yet herself can seem youth's very fountain,
Being all brimmed with life.' 'Were it but true
I would have found the best that life can give,
Companionship in those mysterious things
That make a man's soul or a woman's soul
Itself and not some other soul.' 'That love
Must needs be in this life and in what follows
Unchanging and at peace, and it is right
Every philosopher should praise that love.
But I being none can praise its opposite.

It makes my passion stronger but to think
Like passion stirs the peacock and his mate,
The wild stag and the doe; that mouth to mouth
Is a man's mockery of the changeless soul.'
And thereupon his bounty gave what now
Can shake more blossom from autumnal chill
Than all my bursting springtime knew. A girl
Perched in some window of her mother's house
Had watched my daily passage to and fro;
Had heard impossible history of my past;
Imagined some impossible history
Lived at my side; thought time's disfiguring touch
Gave but more reason for a woman's care.
Yet was it love of me, or was it love
Of the stark mystery that has dazed my sight,
Perplexed her phantasy and planned her care?
Or did the torchlight of that mystery
Pick out my features in such light and shade
Two contemplating passions chose one theme
Through sheer bewilderment? She had not paced
The garden paths, nor counted up the rooms,
Before she had spread a book upon her knees
And asked about the pictures or the text;
And often those first days I saw her stare
On old dry writing in a learned tongue,
On old dry faggots that could never please
The extravagance of spring; or move a hand
As if that writing or the figured page
Were some dear cheek. Upon a moonless night
I sat where I could watch her sleeping form,
And wrote by candle-light; but her form moved,
And fearing that my light disturbed her sleep
I rose that I might screen it with a cloth.
I heard her voice, 'Turn that I may expound
What's bowed your shoulder and made pale your cheek';

And saw her sitting upright on the bed;
Or was it she that spoke or some great Djinn?
I say that a Djinn spoke. A live-long hour
She seemed the learned man and I the child;
Truths without father came, truths that no book
Of all the uncounted books that I have read,
Nor thought out of her mind or mine begot,
Self-born, high-born, and solitary truths,
Those terrible implacable straight lines
Drawn through the wandering vegetative dream,
Even those truths that when my bones are dust
Must drive the Arabian host. The voice grew still,
And she lay down upon her bed and slept,
But woke at the first gleam of day, rose up
And swept the house and sang about her work
In childish ignorance of all that passed.
A dozen nights of natural sleep, and then
When the full moon swam to its greatest height
She rose, and with her eyes shut fast in sleep
Walked through the house. Unnoticed and unfelt
I wrapped her in a heavy hooded cloak, and she,
Half running, dropped at the first ridge of the desert
And there marked out those emblems on the sand
That day by day I study and marvel at,
With her white finger. I led her home asleep
And once again she rose and swept the house
In childish ignorance of all that passed.
Even to-day, after some seven years
When maybe thrice in every moon her mouth
Murmured the wisdom of the desert Djinns,
She keeps that ignorance, nor has she now
That first unnatural interest in my books.
It seems enough that I am there; and yet
Old fellow student, whose most patient ear
Heard all the anxiety of my passionate youth,

It seems I must buy knowledge with my peace.
What if she lose her ignorance and so
Dream that I love her only for the voice,
That every gift and every word of praise
Is but a payment for that midnight voice
That is to age what milk is to a child!
Were she to lose her love, because she had lost
Her confidence in mine, or even lose
Its first simplicity, love, voice and all,
All my fine feathers would be plucked away
And I left shivering. The voice has drawn
A quality of wisdom from her love's
Particular quality. The signs and shapes;
All those abstractions that you fancied were
From the great treatise of Parmenides;
All, all those gyres and cubes and midnight things
Are but a new expression of her body
Drunk with the bitter sweetness of her youth.
And now my utmost mystery is out.
A woman's beauty is a storm-tossed banner;
Under it wisdom stands, and I alone—
Of all Arabia's lovers I alone—
Nor dazzled by the embroidery, nor lost
In the confusion of its night-dark folds,
Can hear the armed man speak.

1923

ALL SOULS' NIGHT

AN EPILOGUE TO 'A VISION'

Midnight has come and the great Christ Church Bell,
And may a lesser bell, sound through the room;
And it is All Souls' Night,
And two long glasses brimmed with muscatel
Bubble upon the table. A ghost may come;
For it is a ghost's right,
His element is so fine
Being sharpened by his death,
To drink from the wine-breath
While our gross palates drink from the whole wine.

I need some mind that, if the cannon sound
From every quarter of the world, can stay
Wound in mind's pondering,
As mummies in the mummy-cloth are wound;
Because I have a marvellous thing to say,
A certain marvellous thing
None but the living mock,
Though not for sober ear;
It may be all that hear
Should laugh and weep an hour upon the clock.

H-'s the first I call. He loved strange thought
And knew that sweet extremity of pride
That's called platonic love,
And that to such a pitch of passion wrought
Nothing could bring him, when his lady died,
Anodyne for his love.
Words were but wasted breath;

One dear hope had he:
The inclemency
Of that or the next winter would be death.

Two thoughts were so mixed up I could not tell
Whether of her or God he thought the most,
But think that his mind's eye,
When upward turned, on one sole image fell;
And that a slight companionable ghost,
Wild with divinity,
Had so lit up the whole
Immense miraculous house
The Bible promised us,
It seemed a gold-fish swimming in a bowl.

On Florence Emery I call the next,
Who finding the first wrinkles on a face
Admired and beautiful,
And knowing that the future would be vexed
With 'minished beauty, multiplied commonplace,
Preferred to teach a school,
Away from neighbour or friend
Among dark skins, and there
Permit foul years to wear
Hidden from eyesight to the unnoticed end.

Before that end much had she ravelled out
From a discourse in figurative speech
By some learned Indian
On the soul's journey. How it is whirled about,
Wherever the orbit of the moon can reach,
Until it plunge into the sun;
And there, free and yet fast
Being both Chance and Choice,
Forget its broken toys
And sink into its own delight at last.

And I call up MacGregor from the grave,
For in my first hard springtime we were friends,
Although of late estranged.
I thought him half a lunatic, half knave,
And told him so, but friendship never ends;
And what if mind seem changed,
And it seem changed with the mind,
When thoughts rise up unbid
On generous things that he did
And I grow half contented to be blind.

He had much industry at setting out,
Much boisterous courage, before loneliness
Had driven him crazed;
For meditations upon unknown thought
Make human intercourse grow less and less;
They are neither paid nor praised.
But he'd object to the host,
The glass because my glass;
A ghost-lover he was
And may have grown more arrogant being a ghost.

But names are nothing. What matter who it be,
So that his elements have grown so fine
The fume of muscatel
Can give his sharpened palate ecstasy
No living man can drink from the whole wine.
I have mummy truths to tell
Whereat the living mock,
Though not for sober ear,
For maybe all that hear
Should laugh and weep an hour upon the clock.

Such thought—such thought have I that hold it tight
Till meditation master all its parts,

Nothing can stay my glance
Until that glance run in the world's despite
To where the damned have howled away their hearts,
And where the blessed dance;
Such thought, that in it bound
I need no other thing
Wound in mind's wandering,
As mummies in the mummy-cloth are wound.

NOTES

SAILING TO BYZANTIUM

Stanza IV

I have read somewhere that in the Emperor's palace at Byzantium was a tree made of gold and silver, and artificial birds that sang.

THE TOWER

Part II

The persons mentioned are associated by legend, story and tradition with the neighbourhood of Thoor Ballylee or Ballylee Castle, where the poem was written. Mrs. French lived at Peterswell in the eighteenth century and was related to Sir Jonah Barrington, who described the incident of the ear and the trouble that came of it. The peasant beauty and the blind poet are Mary Hynes and Raftery, and the incident of the man drowned in Cloone Bog is recorded in my Celtic Twilight. Hanrahan's pursuit of the phantom hare and hounds is from my Stories of Red Hanrahan. The ghosts have been seen at their game of dice in what is now my bedroom, and the old bankrupt man lived about a hundred years ago. According to one legend he could only leave the Castle upon a Sunday because of his creditors, and according to another he hid in the secret passage.

THE TOWER

Part III

In the passage about the Swan I have unconsciously echoed one of the loveliest lyrics of our time—Mr. Sturge Moore's 'Dying Swan'. I often recited it during an American lecturing tour, which explains the theft.

THE DYING SWAN

> O silver-throated Swan
> Struck, struck! A golden dart
> Clean through thy breast has gone
> Home to thy heart.
> Thrill, thrill, O silver throat!
> O silver trumpet, pour
> Love for defiance back
> On him who smote!
> And brim, brim o'er
> With love; and ruby-dye thy track
> Down thy last living reach
> Of river, sail the golden light—
> Enter the sun's heart—even teach,
> O wondrous-gifted pain, teach thou
> The God to love, let him learn how!

When I wrote the lines about Plato and Plotinus I forgot that it is something in our own eyes that makes us see them as all transcendence. Has not Plotinus written: 'Let every soul recall, then, at the outset the truth that soul is the author of all living things, that it has breathed the life into them all, whatever is nourished by earth and sea, all the creatures of the air, the divine stars in the sky; it is the maker of the sun; itself formed and ordered this vast heaven and conducts all that rhythmic motion—and it is a principle distinct from all these to which it gives law and movement and life, and it must of necessity be more honourable than they, for they gather or dissolve as soul brings them life or abandons them, but soul, since it never can abandon itself, is of eternal being'.

MEDITATIONS IN TIME OF CIVIL WAR

These poems were written at Thoor Ballylee in 1922, during the civil war. Before they were finished the Republicans blew up our 'ancient bridge' one midnight. They forbade us to leave the house, but were otherwise polite, even saying at last 'Goodnight, thank you' as though we had given them the bridge.

SECTION SIX

In the West of Ireland we call a starling a stare, and during the civil war one built in a hole in the masonry by my bedroom window.

SECTION SEVEN, STANZA II

The cry 'Vengeance on the murderers of Jacques Molay', Grand Master of the Templars, seems to me fit symbol for those who labour from hatred, and so for sterility in various kinds. It is said to have been incorporated in the ritual of certain Masonic societies of the eighteenth century, and to have fed class-hatred.

SECTION SEVEN, STANZA IV

I have a ring with a hawk and a butterfly upon it, to symbolise the straight road of logic, and so of mechanism, and the crooked road of intuition: 'For wisdom is a butterfly and not a gloomy bird of prey'.

NINETEEN HUNDRED AND NINETEEN

SECTION SIX

The country people see at times certain apparitions whom they name now 'fallen angels', now 'ancient inhabitants of the country', and describe as riding at whiles 'with flowers upon the heads of the horses'. I have assumed in the sixth poem that these horsemen, now that the times worsen, give way to worse. My last symbol, Robert Artisson, was an evil spirit much run after in Kilkenny at the start of the fourteenth century. Are not those who travel in the whirling dust also in the Platonic Year?

TWO SONGS FROM A PLAY

These songs are sung by the Chorus in a play that has for its theme Christ's first appearance to the Apostles after the Resurrection, a play intended for performance in a drawing-room or studio.

AMONG SCHOOL CHILDREN

STANZA III

I have taken 'the honey of generation' from Porphyry's essay on 'The Cave of the Nymphs', but find no warrant in Porphyry for considering it the 'drug' that destroys the 'recollection' of pre-natal freedom. He blamed a cup of oblivion given in the zodiacal sign of Cancer.

THE GIFT OF HARUN AL-RASHID

Part of an unfinished set of poems, dialogues and stories about John Ahern and Michael Robartes, Kusta ben Luka, a philosopher of Bagdad, and his Bedouin followers.

THE HOUR-GLASS

DRAMATIS PERSONAE

A WISE MAN

A FOOL

SOME PUPILS

AN ANGEL

THE WISE MAN'S WIFE AND TWO CHILDREN

SCENE: *A large room with a door at the back and another at the side opening to an inner room. A desk and a chair in the middle. An hour-glass on a bracket near the door. A creepy stool near it. Some benches. The Wise Man sitting at his desk.*

WISE MAN [*turning over the pages of a book*]. Where is that passage I am to explain to my pupils to-day? Here it is, and the book says that it was written by a beggar on the walls of Babylon: "There are two living countries, the one visible and the one invisible; and when it is winter with us it is summer in that country; and when the November winds are up among us it is lambing-time there." I wish that my pupils had asked me to explain any other passage, for this is a hard passage. [*The fool comes in and stands at the door, holding out his hat. He has a pair of shears in the other hand.*] It sounds to me like foolishness; and yet that cannot be, for the writer of this book, where I have found so much knowledge, would not have set it by itself on this page, and surrounded it with so many images and so many deep colors and so much fine gilding, if it had been foolishness.

FOOL. Give me a penny.

WISE MAN. [*Turns to another page.*] Here he has written: "The learned in old times forgot the visible country." That I understand, but I have taught my learners better.

FOOL. Won't you give me a penny?

WISE MAN. What do you want? The words of the wise Saracen will not teach you much.

FOOL. Such a great wise teacher as you are will not refuse a penny to a Fool.

WISE MAN. What do you know about wisdom?

FOOL. Oh, I know! I know what I have seen.

WISE MAN. What is it you have seen?

FOOL. When I went by Kilcluan where the bells used to be ringing at the break of every day, I could hear nothing but the people snoring in their houses. When I went by Tubbervanach where the young men used to be climbing the hill to the blessed well, they were sitting at the crossroads playing cards. When I went by Carrigoras where the friars used to be fasting and serving the poor, I saw them drinking wine and obeying their wives. And when I asked what misfortune had brought all these changes, they said it was no misfortune, but it was the wisdom they had learned from your teaching.

WISE MAN. Run round to the kitchen, and my wife will give you something to eat.

FOOL. That is foolish advice for a wise man to give.

WISE MAN. Why, Fool?

FOOL. What is eaten is gone. I want pennies for my bag. I must buy bacon in the shops, and nuts in the market, and strong drink for the time when the sun is weak. And I want snares to catch the rabbits and the squirrels and the bares, and a pot to cook them in.

WISE MAN. Go away. I have other things to think of now than giving you pennies.

FOOL. Give me a penny and I will bring you luck. Bresal the Fisherman lets me sleep among the nets in his loft in the winter-

time because he says I bring him luck; and in the summer-time
the wild creatures let me sleep near their nests and their holes. It
is lucky even to look at me or to touch me, but it is much more
lucky to give me a penny. [*Holds out his hand.*] If I wasn't lucky,
I'd starve.

WISE MAN. What have you got the shears for?

FOOL. I won't tell you. If I told you, you would drive them
away.

WISE MAN. Whom would I drive away?

FOOL. I won't tell you.

WISE MAN. Not if I give you a penny?

FOOL. No.

WISE MAN. Not if I give you two pennies.

FOOL. You will be very lucky if you give me two pennies,
but I won't tell you.

WISE MAN. Three pennies?

FOOL. Four, and I will tell you!

WISE MAN. Very well, four. But I will not call you Teigue
the Fool any longer.

FOOL. Let me come close to you where nobody will hear
me. But first you must promise you will not drive them away.
[*WISE MAN nods.*] Every day men go out dressed in black and
spread great black nets over the hill, great black nets.

WISE MAN. Why do they do that?

FOOL. That they may catch the feet of the angels. But every

morning, just before the dawn, I go out and cut the nets with my shears, and the angels fly away.

WISE MAN. Ah, now I know that you are Teigue the Fool. You have told me that I am wise, and I have never seen an angel.

FOOL. I have seen plenty of angels.

WISE MAN. Do you bring luck to the angels too.

FOOL. Oh, no, no! No one could do that. But they are always there if one looks about one; they are like the blades of grass.

WISE MAN. When do you see them?

FOOL. When one gets quiet; then something wakes up inside one, something happy and quiet like the stars—not like the seven that move, but like the fixed stars. [*He points upward.*]

WISE MAN. And what happens then?

FOOL. Then all in a minute one smells summer flowers, and tall people go by, happy and laughing, and their clothes are the color of burning sods.

WISE MAN. Is it long since you have seen them, Teigue the Fool?

FOOL. Not long, glory be to God! I saw one coming behind me just now. It was not laughing, but it had clothes the color of burning sods, and there was something shining about its head.

WISE MAN. Well, there are your four pennies. You, a fool, say "Glory be to God," but before I came the wise men said it. Run away now. I must ring the bell for my scholars.

FOOL. Four pennies! That means a great deal of luck. Great

teacher, I have brought you plenty of luck! [*He goes out shaking the bag.*]

WISE MAN. Though they call him Teigue the Fool, he is not more foolish than everybody used to be, with their dreams and their preachings and their three worlds; but I have overthrown their three worlds with the seven sciences. [*He touches the books with his hands.*] With Philosophy that was made for the lonely star, I have taught them to forget Theology; with Architecture, I have hidden the ramparts of their cloudy heaven; with Music, the fierce planets' daughter whose hair is always on fire, and with Grammar that is the moon's daughter, I have shut their ears to the imaginary harpings and speech of the angels; and I have made formations of battle with Arithmetic that have put the hosts of heaven to the rout. But, Rhetoric and Dialectic, that have been born out of the light star and out of the amorous star, you have been my spearman and my catapult! Oh! my swift horseman! Oh! my keen darting arguments, it is because of you that I have overthrown the hosts of foolishness! [*An Angel, in a dress the color of embers, and carrying a blossoming apple bough in his hand and with a gilded halo about his head, stands upon the threshold.*] Before I came, men's minds were stuffed with folly about a heaven where birds sang the hours, and about angels that came and stood upon men's thresholds. But I have locked the visions into heaven and turned the key upon them. Well, I must consider this passage about the two countries. My mother used to say something of the kind. She would say that when our bodies sleep our souls awake, and that whatever withers here ripens yonder, and that harvests are snatched from us that they may feed invisible people. But the meaning of the book must be different, for only fools and women have thoughts like that; their thoughts were never written upon the walls of Babylon. [*He sees the Angel.*] What are you? Who are you? I think I saw some that were like you in my dreams when I was a child—that bright thing, that dress that is the color of embers! But I have done with dreams, I have done with dreams.

ANGEL. I am the Angel of the Most High God.

WISE MAN. Why have you come to me?

ANGEL. I have brought you a message.

WISE MAN. What message have you got for me?

ANGEL. You will die within the hour. You will die when the last grains have fallen in this glass. [*He turns the hour-glass.*]

WISE MAN. My time to die has not come. I have my pupils. I have a young wife and children that I cannot leave. Why must I die?

ANGEL. You must die because no souls have passed over the threshold of heaven since you came into this country. The threshold is grassy, and the gates are rusty, and the angels that keep watch there are lonely.

WISE MAN. Where will death bring me to?

ANGEL. The doors of heaven will not open to you, for you have denied the existence of heaven; and the doors of purgatory will not open to you, for you have denied the existence of purgatory.

WISE MAN. But I have also denied the existence of hell!

ANGEL. Hell is the place of those who deny.

WISE MAN [*kneeling*]. I have indeed denied everything and have taught others to deny. I have believed in nothing but what my senses told me. But, oh! beautiful Angel, forgive me, forgive me!

ANGEL. You should have asked forgiveness long ago.

WISE MAN. Had I seen your face as I see it now, oh!

beautiful Angel, I would have believed, I would have asked forgiveness. Maybe you do not know how easy it is to doubt. Storm, death, the grass rotting, many sicknesses, those are the messengers that came to me. Oh! why are you silent? You carry the pardon of the Most High; give it to me! I would kiss your hands if I were not afraid— no, no, the hem of your dress!

ANGEL. You let go undying hands too long ago to take hold of them now.

WISE MAN. You cannot understand. You live in that country people only see in their dreams. You live in a country that we can only dream about. Maybe it is as hard for you to understand why we disbelieve as it is for us to believe. Oh! what have I said! You know everything! Give me time to undo what I have done. Give me a year—a month—a day—an hour! Give me this hour's end, that I may undo what I have done!

ANGEL. You cannot undo what you have done. Yet I have this power with my message. If you can find one that believes before the hour's end, you shall come to heaven after the years of purgatory. For, from one fiery seed, watched over by those that sent me, the harvest can come again to heap the golden threshing-floor. But now farewell, for I am weary of the weight of time.

WISE MAN. Blessed be the Father, blessed be the Son, blessed be the Spirit, blessed be the Messenger They have sent!

ANGEL [*at the door and pointing at the hour-glass*]. In a little while the uppermost glass will be empty. [*Goes out.*]

WISE MAN. Everything will be well with me. I will call my pupils; they only say they doubt. [*Pulls the bell.*] They will be here in a moment. I hear their feet outside on the path. They want to please me; they pretend that they disbelieve. Belief is too old to be overcome all in a minute. Besides, I can prove what I once disproved. [*Another pull at the bell.*] They are coming now. I will go to my desk. I will speak quietly, as if nothing had happened.

[He stands at the desk with a fixed look in his eyes.]

[Enter Pupils and the Fool.]

FOOL. Leave me alone. Leave me alone. Who is that pulling at my bag? King's son, do not pull at my bag.

A YOUNG MAN. Did your friends the angels give you that bag? Why don't they fill your bag for you?

FOOL. Give me pennies! Give me some pennies!

A YOUNG MAN. Let go his cloak, it is coming to pieces. What do you want pennies for, with that great bag at your waist?

FOOL. I want to buy bacon in the shops, and nuts in the market, and strong drink for the time when the sun is weak, and snares to catch rabbits and the squirrels that steal the nuts, and hares, and a great pot to cook them in.

A YOUNG MAN. Why don't your friends tell you where buried treasures are?

ANOTHER. Why don't they make you dream about treasures? If one dreams three times, there is always treasure.

FOOL [*holding out his hat*]. Give me pennies! Give me pennies!

[*They throw pennies into his hat. He is standing close to the door, that he may hold out his hat to each newcomer.*]

A YOUNG MAN. Master, will you have Teigue the Fool for a scholar?

ANOTHER YOUNG MAN. Teigue, will you give us pennies if we teach you lessons? No, he goes to school for nothing on the mountains. Tell us what you learn on the mountains, Teigue?

WISE MAN. Be silent all. [*He has been standing silent, looking away.*] Stand still in your places, for there is something I would have you tell me.

[*A moment's pause. They all stand round in their places. Teigue still stands at the door.*]

WISE MAN. Is there any one amongst you who believes in God? In heaven? Or in purgatory? Or in hell?

ALL THE YOUNG MEN. No one; Master! No one!

WISE MAN. I knew you would all say that; but do not be afraid. I will not be angry. Tell me the truth. Do you not believe?

A YOUNG MAN. We once did, but you have taught us to know better.

WISE MAN. Oh! teaching, teaching does not go very deep! The heart remains unchanged under it all. You believe just as you always did, and you are afraid to tell me.

A YOUNG MAN. No, no, master.

WISE MAN. If you tell me that you believe I shall be glad and not angry.

A YOUNG MAN. [*To his neighbor.*] He wants somebody to dispute with.

HIS NEIGHBOR. I knew that from the beginning.

A YOUNG MAN. That is not the subject for to-day; you were going to talk about the words the beggar wrote upon the walls of Babylon.

WISE MAN. If there is one amongst you that believes, he will be my best friend. Surely there is one amongst you. [*They are all silent.*] Surely what you learned at your mother's knees has not been so soon forgotten.

A YOUNG MAN. Master, till you came, no teacher in this land was able to get rid of foolishness and ignorance. But every one has listened to you, every one has learned the truth. You have had your last disputation.

ANOTHER. What a fool you made of that monk in the market-place! He had not a word to say.

WISE MAN. [*Comes from his desk and stands among them in the middle of the room.*] Pupils, dear friends, I have deceived you all this time. It was I myself who was ignorant. There is a God. There is a heaven. There is fire that passes, and there is fire that lasts for ever.

[*Teigue, through all this, is sitting on a stool by the door, reckoning on his fingers what he will buy with his money.*]

A YOUNG MAN [*to another*]. He will not be satisfied till we dispute with him. [*To the Wise Man.*] Prove it, master. Have you seen them?

WISE MAN [*in a low, solemn voice*]. Just now, before you came in, some one came to the door, and when I looked up I saw an angel standing there.

A YOUNG MAN. You were in a dream. Anybody can see an angel in his dreams.

WISE MAN. Oh, my God! it was not a dream. I was awake, waking as I am now. I tell you I was awake as I am now.

A YOUNG MAN. Some dream when they are awake, but they are the crazy, and who would believe what they say?

Forgive me, master, but that is what you taught me to say. That is what you said to the monk when he spoke of the visions of the saints and the martyrs.

ANOTHER YOUNG MAN. You see how well we remember your teaching.

WISE MAN. Out, out from my sight! I want some one with belief. I must find that grain the Angel spoke of before I die. I tell you I must find it, and you answer me with arguments. Out with you, or I will beat you with my stick! [*The young men laugh.*]

A YOUNG MAN. How well he plays at faith! He is like the monk when he had nothing more to say.

WISE MAN. Out, out, or I will lay this stick about your shoulders! Out with you, though you are a king's son!

[*They begin to hurry out.*]

A YOUNG MAN. Come, come; he wants us to find some one who will dispute with him. [*All go out.*]

WISE MAN [*alone. He goes to the door at the side*]. I will call my wife. She will believe; women always believe. [*He opens the door and calls.*] Bridget! Bridget! [*Bridget comes in wearing her apron, her sleeves turned up from her floury arms.*] Bridget, tell me the truth; do not say what you think will please me. Do you sometimes say your prayers?

BRIDGET. Prayers! No, you taught me to leave them off long ago. At first I was sorry, but I am glad now, for I am sleepy in the evenings.

WISE MAN. But do you not believe in God?

BRIDGET. Oh, a good wife only believes what her husband tells her!

WISE MAN. But sometimes when you are alone, when I am in the school and the children asleep, do you not think about the saints, about the things you used to believe in? What do you think of when you are alone?

BRIDGET [*considering*]. I think about nothing. Sometimes I wonder if the pig is fattening well, or I go out to see if the crows are picking up the chickens' food.

WISE MAN. Oh, what can I do! Is there nobody who believes? I must go and find somebody! [*He goes toward the door but with his eyes fixed on the hour-glass.*] I cannot go out; I cannot leave that!

BRIDGET. You want somebody to get up argument with.

WISE MAN. Oh, look out of the door and tell me if there is anybody there in the street. I cannot leave this glass; somebody might shake it! Then the sand would fall quickly.

BRIDGET. I don't understand what you are saying. [*Looks out.*] There is a crowd of people talking to your pupils.

WISE MAN. Oh, run out, Bridget, and see if they have found somebody that believes!

BRIDGET [*wiping her arms in her apron and pulling down her sleeves*]. It's a hard thing to be married to a man of learning that must be always having arguments. [*Goes out and shouts through the kitchen door.*] Don't be meddling with the bread, children, while I'm out.

WISE MAN. [*Kneels down.*] "Salvum me fac, Deus—salvum—salvum...." I have forgotten it all. It is thirty years since I said a prayer. I must pray in the common tongue, like a clown begging in the market like Teigue the Fool! [*He prays.*] Help me, Father, Son, and Spirit!

[*Bridget enters, followed by the Fool, who is holding out his hat to her.*]

FOOL. Give me something; give me a penny to buy bacon in the shops, and nuts in the market, and strong drink for the time when the sun grows weak.

BRIDGET. I have no pennies. [*To the Wise Man.*] Your pupils cannot find anybody to argue with you. There is nobody in the whole country who had enough belief to fill a pipe with since you put down the monk. Can't you be quiet now and not always be wanting to have arguments? It must be terrible to have a mind like that.

WISE MAN. I am lost! I am lost!

BRIDGET. Leave me alone now; I have to make the bread for you and the children.

WISE MAN. Out of this, woman, out of this, I say! [*Bridget goes through the kitchen door.*] Will nobody find a way to help me! But she spoke of my children. I had forgotten them. They will believe. It is only those who have reason that doubt; the young are full of faith. Bridget, Bridget, send my children to me!

BRIDGET [*inside*]. Your father wants you, run to him now.

[*The two children came in. They stand together a little way from the threshold of the kitchen door, looking timidly at their father.*]

WISE MAN. Children, what do you believe? Is there a heaven? Is there a hell? Is there a purgatory?

FIRST CHILD. We haven't forgotten, father.

THE OTHER CHILD. Oh, no, father. [*They both speak together as if in school.*] There is no heaven; there is no hell; there is nothing we cannot see.

FIRST CHILD. Foolish people used to think that there were, but you are very learned and you have taught us better.

WISE MAN. You are just as bad as the others, just as bad as the others! Out of the room with you, out of the room! [*The children begin to cry and run away.*] Go away, go away! I will teach you better—no, I will never teach you again. Go to your mother—no, she will not be able to teach them.... Help them, O God! [*Alone.*] The grains are going very quickly. There is very little sand in the uppermost glass. Somebody will come for me in a moment; perhaps he is at the door now! All creatures that have reason doubt. O that the grass and the planets could speak! Somebody has said that they would wither if they doubted. O speak to me, O grass blades! O fingers of God's certainty, speak to me. You are millions and you will not speak. I dare not know the moment the messenger will come for me. I will cover the glass. [*He covers it and brings it to the desk, and the Fool, is sitting by the door fiddling with some flowers which he has stuck in his hat. He has begun to blow a dandelion head.*] What are you doing?

FOOL. Wait a moment. [*He blows.*] Four, five, six.

WISE MAN. What are you doing that for?

FOOL. I am blowing at the dandelion to find out what time it is.

WISE MAN. You have heard everything! That is why you want to find out what hour it is! You are waiting to see them coming through the door to carry me away. [*Fool goes on blowing.*] Out through the door with you! I will have no one here when they come. [*He seizes the Fool by the shoulders, and begins to force him out through the door, then suddenly changes his mind.*] No, I have something to ask you. [*He drags him back into the room.*] Is there a heaven? Is there a hell? Is there a purgatory?

FOOL. So you ask me now. I thought when you were asking

your pupils, I said to myself, if he would ask Teigue the Fool, Teigue could tell him all about it, for Teigue has learned all about it when he has been cutting the nets.

WISE MAN. Tell me; tell me!

FOOL. I said, Teigue knows everything. Not even the owls and the hares that milk the cows have Teigue's wisdom. But Teigue will not speak; he says nothing.

WISE MAN. Tell me, tell me! For under the cover the grains are falling, and when they are all fallen I shall die; and my soul will be lost if I have not found somebody that believes! Speak, speak!

FOOL [*looking wise*]. No, no, I won't tell you what is in my mind, and I won't tell you what is in my bag. You might steal away my thoughts. I met a bodach on the road yesterday, and he said, "Teigue, tell me how many pennies are in your bag. I will wager three pennies that there are not twenty pennies in your bag; let me put in my hand and count them." But I pulled the strings tighter, like this; and when I go to sleep every night I hide the bag where no one knows.

WISE MAN. [*Goes toward the hour-glass as if to uncover it.*] No, no, I have not the courage! [*He kneels.*] Have pity upon me, Fool, and tell me!

FOOL. Ah! Now, that is different. I am not afraid of you now. But I must come near you; somebody in there might hear what the Angel said.

WISE MAN. Oh, what did the Angel tell you?

FOOL. Once I was alone on the hills, and an Angel came by and he said, "Teigue the Fool, do not forget the Three Fires: the Fire that punishes, the Fire that purifies, and the Fire wherein the soul rejoices for ever!"

WISE MAN. He believes! I am saved! Help me. The sand has run out. I am dying.... [*Fool helps him to his chair.*] I am going from the country of the seven wandering stars, and I am going to the country of the fixed stars! Ring the bell. [*Fool rings the bell.*] Are they coming? Ah! now I hear their feet.... I will speak to them. I understand it all now. One sinks in on God: we do not see the truth; God sees the truth in us. I cannot speak, I am too weak. Tell them, Fool, that when the life and the mind are broken, the truth comes through them like peas through a broken peascod. But no, I will pray—yet I cannot pray. Pray Fool, that they may be given a sign and save their souls alive. Your prayers are better than mine.

[*Fool bows his head. Wise Man's head sinks on his arm on the books.*
Pupils enter.]

A YOUNG MAN. Look at the Fool turned bell-ringer!

ANOTHER. What have you called us in for, Teigue? What are you going to tell us?

ANOTHER. No wonder he has had dreams! See, he is fast asleep now. [*Goes over and touches the Wise Man.*] Oh, he is dead!

FOOL. Do not stir! He asked for a sign that you might be saved. [*All are silent for a moment.*] Look what has come from his mouth... a little winged thing... a little shining thing. It has gone to the door. [*The Angel appears in the doorway, stretches out her hands and closes them again.*] The Angel has taken it in her hands... she will open her hands in the Garden of Paradise.

[*They all kneel.*]

MOSADA

"And my Lord Cardinal hath had strange days in his youth."

Extract from a Memoir of the Fifteenth Century.

SCENE I

A Little Moorish Room in the Village of Azubia.
In the centre of the room a chafing dish.

Mosada [*alone*]

Three times the roses have grown less
and less,
As slowly Autumn climbed the golden throne
Where sat old Summer fading into song,
And thrice the peaches flushed upon the walls,
And thrice the corn around the sickles flamed,
Since 'mong my people, tented on the hills,
He stood a messenger. In April's prime
(Swallows were flashing their white breasts above
Or perching on the tents, a-weary still
From waste seas cross'd, yet ever garrulous)
Along the velvet vale I saw him come:
In Autumn, when far down the mountain slopes
The heavy clusters of the grapes were full,
I saw him sigh and turn and pass away;
For I and all my people were accurst
Of his sad God; and down among the grass
Hiding my face, I cried long, bitterly.
Twas evening, and the cricket nation sang
Around my head and danced among the grass;
And all was dimness till a dying leaf
Slid circling down and softly touched my lips
With dew as though 'twere sealing them for death.
Yet somewhere in the footsore world we meet
We two before we die, for Azolar
The star-taught Moor said thus it was decreed

89

By those wan stars that sit in company
Above the Alpujarras on their thrones,
That when the stars of our nativity
Draw star to star, as on that eve he passed
Down the long valleys from my people's tents,
We meet—we two.

[*She opens the casement—the mingled sound of the voices and laughter
of the apple gatherers floats in.*]

How merry all these are
Among the fruit. But yon, lame Cola crouches
Away from all the others. Now the sun—
A-shining on the little crucifix
Of silver hanging round lame Cola's neck—
Sinks down at last with yonder minaret
Of the Alhambra black athwart his disk;
And Cola seeing, knows the sign and comes.
Thus do I burn these precious herbs whose smoke
Pours up and floats in fragrance o'er my head
In coil on coil of azure.

[*Enter Cola.*] All is ready.

Cola

Mosada, it is then so much the worse.
I will not share your sin.

Mosada

It is no sin
That you shall see on yonder glowing cloud
Pictured, where wander the beloved feet
Whose footfall I have longed for, three sad summers—
Why these new fears?

Cola

The servant of the Lord,
The dark still man, has come, and says 'tis sin.

Mosada

They say the wish itself is half the sin.
Then has this one been sinned full many times,
Yet 'tis no sin—my father taught it me.
He was a man most learned and most mild,
Who, dreaming to a wondrous age, lived on
Tending the roses round his lattice door.
For years his days had dawned and faded thus
Among the plants; the flowery silence fell
Deep in his soul, like rain upon a soil
Worn by the solstice fierce, and made it pure.
Would he teach any sin?

Cola

Gaze in the cloud
Yourself.

Mosada

None but the innocent can see.

Cola

They say I am all ugliness; lame-footed
I am; one shoulder turned awry—why then
Should I be good? But you are beautiful.

Mosada

I cannot see.

Cola

The beetles, and the bats,
And spiders, are my friends, I'm theirs, and they are
Not good; but you are like the butterflies.

Mosada

I cannot see! I cannot see! but you
Shall see a thing to talk on when you're old,
Under a lemon tree beside your door;
And all the elders sitting in the sun,
Will wondering listen, and this tale shall ease
For long, the burthen of their talking griefs.

Cola

Upon my knees I pray you, let it sleep,
The vision.

Mosada

You're pale and weeping, child.
Be not afraid, you'll see no fearful thing.
Thus, thus I beckon from her viewless fields—
Thus beckon to our aid a Phantom fair
And calm, robed all in raiment moony white.
She was a great enchantress once of yore,
Whose dwelling was a tree-wrapt island, lulled
Far out upon the water world and ringed
With wonderful white sand, where never yet

Were furled the wings of ships. There in a dell
A lily blanchèd place, she sat and sang,
And in her singing wove around her head
White lilies, and her song flew forth afar
Along the sea; and many a man grew hushed
In his own house or 'mong the merchants grey,
Hearing the far off singing guile and groaned,
And manned an argosy and sailing died.
In the far isle she sang herself asleep
At last. But now I wave her to my side.

Cola

Stay, stay, or I will hold your white arms down.
Ah me, I cannot reach them—here and there
Darting you wave them, darting in the vapour.
Heard you? Your lute upon the wall has sounded!
I feel a finger drawn across my cheek!

Mosada

The phantoms come; ha ha! they come, they come!
I wave them hither, my breast heaves with joy.
Ah! now I'm eastern-hearted once again,
And while they gather round my beckoning arms,
I'll sing the songs the dusky lovers sing,
Wandering in sultry palaces of Ind,
A lotus in their hands—

[*The door is flung open. Enter the Officers of the Inquisition.*]

First Inquisitor

Young Moorish girl
Taken in magic. In the Church's name
I here arrest thee.

Mosada

It is Allah's will.
Touch not this boy, for he is innocent.

Cola

Forgive! for I have told them everything.
They said I'd burn in hell unless I told
Them all, and let them find you in the vapour.

[*She turns away—he clings to her dress.*]

Forgive me!

Mosada

It was Allah's will.

Second Inquisitor

Now cords.

Mosada

No need to bind my hands. Where are ye, sirs,
For ye are hid with vapours?

Second Inquisitor

Round the stake
The vapour is much thicker.

Cola

God! the stake!

Ye said that ye would fright her from her sin—
No more; take me instead of her, great sirs.
She was my only friend; I'm lame you know—
One shoulder twisted, and the children cry
Names after me.

First Inquisitor

Lady—

Mosada

I come.

Cola[*following.*]

Forgive.
Forgive, or I will die.

Mosada [*stooping and kissing him*].

'Twas Allah's will.

SCENE II

A Room, the building of the Inquisition of Granada, lit by stained window, picturing St. James of Spain.

Monks and Inquisitors.

First Monk

Will you not hear my last new song?

First Inquisitor

Hush, hush!
So she must burn you say.

Second Inquisitor

She must in truth.

First Inquisitor

Will he not spare her life? How would one matter
When there are many?

Second Monk

Ebremar will stamp
This heathen horde away. You need not hope;
And know you not she kissed that pious child
With poisonous lips, and he is pining since?

First Monk

You're full of wordiness. Come, hear my song.

Second Monk

In truth an evil race; why strive for her,
A little Moorish girl?

Second Inquisitor

Small worth.

First Monk

My song—

First Inquisitor

I had a sister like her once my friend.

> *[Touching the first Monk on the shoulder.]*

Where is our brother Peter? When you're nigh,
He is not far. I'd have him speak for her.
I saw his jovial mood bring once a smile
To sainted Ebremar's sad eyes. I think
He loves our brother Peter in his heart.
If Peter would but ask her life—who knows?

First Monk

He digs his cabbages. He brings to mind
That song I've made—is of a Russian tale
Of Holy Peter of the Burning Gate:
A saint of Russia in a vision saw

[Sings]

> A stranger new arisen wait
> By the door of Peter's gate,
> And he shouted Open wide
> Thy sacred door, but Peter cried,
> No, thy home is deepest hell,
> Deeper than the deepest well.
> Then the stranger softly crew
> Cock-a-doodle-doodle-doo!
> Answered Peter: Enter in
> Friend; but 'twere a deadly sin
> Ever more to speak a word
> Of any unblessed earthly bird.

First Inquisitor

Be still, I hear the step of Ebremar.
Yonder he comes; bright-eyed, and hollow-cheeked
From fasting—see, the red light slanting down
From the great painted window wraps his brow,
As with an aureole.

[Ebremar enters—they all bow to him.]

First Inquisitor

My suit to you—

Ebremar

I will not hear; the Moorish girl must die.
I will burn heresy from this mad earth,
And—

98

First Inquisitor

Mercy is the manna of the world.

Ebremar

The wages of sin is death.

Second Monk

No use.

First Inquisitor

My lord, if it must be, I pray descend
Yourself into the dungeon 'neath our feet
And importune with weighty words this Moor,
That she foreswear her heresies and save
Her soul from seas of endless flame in hell.

Ebremar

I speak alone with servants of the Cross
And dying men—and yet—but no, farewell.

Second Monk

No use.

Ebremar

Away! [*They go.*] Hear oh! thou enduring God,
Who giveth to the golden-crested wren
Her hanging mansion. Give to me, I pray,
The burthen of thy truth. Reach down thy hands

99

And fill me with thy rage, that I may bruise
The heathen. Yea, and shake the sullen kings
Upon their thrones. The lives of men shall flow
As quiet as the little rivulets
Beneath the sheltering shadow of thy Church,
And thou shalt bend, enduring God, the knees
Of the great warriors whose names have sung
The world to its fierce infancy again.

SCENE III

*The dungeon of the Inquisition. The morning of the Auto-da-Fe
dawns dimly through a barred window. A few faint stars are shining.
Swallows are circling in the dimness without.*

Mosada

Oh! swallows, swallows, swallows, will ye fly
This eve, to-morrow, or to-morrow night
Above the farm-house by the little lake
That's rustling in the reeds with patient pushes,
Soft as a long dead footstep whispering through

The brain

My brothers will be passing down
Quite soon the cornfield, where the poppies grow,
To their farm-work; how silent all will be.
But no, in this warm weather, 'mong the hills,
Will be the faint far thunder-sound as though
The world were dreaming in its summer sleep;
That will be later, day is scarcely dawning.
And Hassan will be with them—he was so small,
A weak, thin child, when last I saw him there.
He will be taller now—'twas long ago.

The men are busy in the glimmering square.
I hear the murmur as they raise the beams
To build the circling seats, where high in air
Soon will the churchmen nod above the crowd.
I'm not of that pale company whose feet
Ere long shall falter through the noisy square,

101

And not come thence—for here in this small ring,
Hearken, ye swallows! I have hoarded up
A poison drop. The toy of fancy once,
A fashion with us Moorish maids, begot
Of dreaming and of watching by the door
The shadows pass; but now, I love my ring,
For it alone of all the world will do
My bidding.

[Sucks poison from the ring.]

Now 'tis done, and I am glad
And free—'twill thieve away with sleepy mood
My thoughts, and yonder brightening patch of sky
With three bars crossed, and these four walls my world,
And yon few stars, grown dim like eyes of lovers
The noisy world divides. How soon a deed
So small makes one grow weak and tottering.
Where shall I lay me down? That question is
A weighty question, for it is the last.
Not there, for there a spider weaves her web.
Nay here, I'll lay me down where I can watch
The burghers of the night fade one by one,
... Yonder a leaf
Of apple blossom circles in the gloom,
Floating from yon barred window. New comer,
Thou'rt welcome. Lie there close against my fingers.
I wonder which is whitest, they or thou.
'Tis thou, for they've grown blue around the nails.
My blossom, I am dying, and the stars
Are dying too. They were full seven stars;
Two only now they are, two side by side.
Oh! Allah, it was thus they shone that night,
When my lost lover left these arms. My Vallence,
We meet at last, the ministering stars

102

Of our nativity hang side by side,
And throb within the circles of green dawn.
Too late, too late, for I am near to death.
I try to lift mine arms—they fall again.
This death is heavy in my veins like sleep.
I cannot even crawl along the flags
A little nearer those bright stars. Tell me,
Is it your message, stars, that when death comes
My soul shall touch with his, and the two flames
Be one? I think all's finished now and sealed.

[*After a pause enter Ebremar.*]

Ebremar

Young Moorish girl, thy final hour is here,
Cast off thy heresies and save thy soul
From dateless pain. She sleeps—

[*Starting.*]

Mosada—thou—
Oh God!—awake, thou shalt not die. She sleeps.
Her head cast backward in her unloosed hair.
Look up, look up, thy Vallence is by thee.
A fearful paleness creeps across her breast
And out-spread arms.

[*Casting himself down by her.*]

Be not so pale, dear love.
Oh! can my kisses bring a flush no more
Upon thy face. How heavily thy head
Hangs on my breast. Listen, we shall be safe.
We'll fly from this before the morning star.

Dear heart, there is a secret way that leads
Its paven length towards the river's marge,
Where lies a shallop in the yellow reeds.
Awake, awake, and we will sail afar,
Afar along the fleet white river's face—
Alone with our own whispers and replies—
Alone among the murmurs of the dawn.
Among thy nation none shall know that I
Was Ebremar, whose thoughts were fixed on God,
And heaven, and holiness.

Mosada

Let's talk and grieve,
For that's the sweetest music for sad souls.
Day's dead, all flame-bewildered, and the hills
In list'ning silence gazing on our grief.
I never knew an eve so marvellous still.

Ebremar

Her dreams are talking with old years. Awake,
Grieve not, for Vallence kneels beside thee—

Mosada

Vallence,
'Tis late, wait one more day; below the hills
The foot-worn way is long, and it grows dark.
It is the darkest eve I ever knew.

Ebremar

I kneel by thee—no parting now—look up.
She smiles—is happy with her wandering griefs.

Mosada

So you must go; kiss me before you go.
Oh! would the busy minutes might fold up
Their thieving wings that we might never part.
I never knew a night so honey sweet.

Ebremar

There is no leave taking. I go no more.
Safe on the breast of Vallence is thy head
Unhappy one.

Mosada

Go not. Go not. Go not.
For night comes fast; look down on me, my love,
And see how thick the dew lies on my face.
I never knew a night so dew-bedrowned.

Ebremar

Oh! hush the wandering music of thy mind.
Look on me once. Why sink your eyelids so?
Why do you hang so heavy in my arms?
Love, will you die when we have met? One look
Give to thy Vallence.

Mosada

Vallence—he has gone
From here, along the shadowy way that winds
Companioning the river's pilgrim torch.
I'll see him longer if I stand out here
Upon the mountain's brow.

*[She tries to stand and totters. Ebremar supports her, and
she stands pointing down as if into a visionary valley.]*

Yonder he treads
The path o'er-muffled with the leaves—dead leaves,
Like happy thoughts grown sad in evil days.
He fades among the mists; how fast they come,
And pour upon the world! Ah! well a day!
Poor love and sorrow with their arms thrown round
Each other's necks, and whispering as they go,
Still wander through the world. He's gone, he's gone.
I'm weary—weary, and 'tis very cold.
I'll draw my cloak around me; it is cold.
I never knew a night so bitter cold.

[Dies.]

Ebremar

Mosada! Oh, Mosada!

[Enter Monks and Inquisitors.]

First Inquisitor

My lord, you called.

Ebremar

Not I. This maid is dead.

First Monk

From poison, for you cannot trust these Moors.
You're pale, my lord.

First Inquisitor [*aside*]

His lips are quivering.
The flame that shone within his eyes but now
Has flickered and gone out.

Ebremar

I am not well.
'Twill pass. I'll see the other prisoners now,
And importune their souls to penitence,
So they escape from hell. But pardon me.
Your hood is threadbare—see that it be changed
Before we take our seats above the crowd.

First Monk

 I always said you could not trust these Moors.
[*They go.*]

THE END